McCordsville Elementary
Media Center

Dogs

Labradors

by Connie Colwell Miller

Consulting Editor: Gail Saunders-Smith, PhD

Consultant: Jennifer Zablotny, DVM
Member, American Veterinary Medical Association

Capstone
press

Mankato, Minnesota

Pebble Books are published by Capstone Press,
151 Good Counsel Drive, P.O. Box 669, Mankato, Minnesota 56002.
www.capstonepress.com

1 2 3 4 5 6 12 11 10 09 08 07

Library of Congress Cataloging-in-Publication Data
Miller, Connie Colwell, 1976–
    Labradors / by Connie Colwell Miller.
    p. cm.—(Pebble Books. Dogs)
    Summary: "Simple text and photographs present the Labrador breed and how
to care for them"—Provided by publisher.
    Includes bibliographical references and index.
    ISBN-13: 978-0-7368-6699-6 (hardcover)
    ISBN-10: 0-7368-6699-X (hardcover)
    1. Labrador retriever—Juvenile literature. I. Title. II. Series.
SF429.L3M55 2007
636.752'7—dc22   2006020448

Note to Parents and Teachers

The Dogs set supports national science standards related to life
science. This book describes and illustrates Labradors. The images
support early readers in understanding the text. The repetition of
words and phrases helps early readers learn new words. This book
also introduces early readers to subject-specific vocabulary words,
which are defined in the Glossary section. Early readers may need
assistance to read some words and to use the Table of Contents,
Glossary, Read More, Internet Sites, and Index sections of the book.

Table of Contents

Loyal Labs

Labradors are
friendly, loyal pets.
People call them "Labs"
for short.

6

Some Labs are
hunting dogs.
They splash into the water
to fetch ducks and geese.

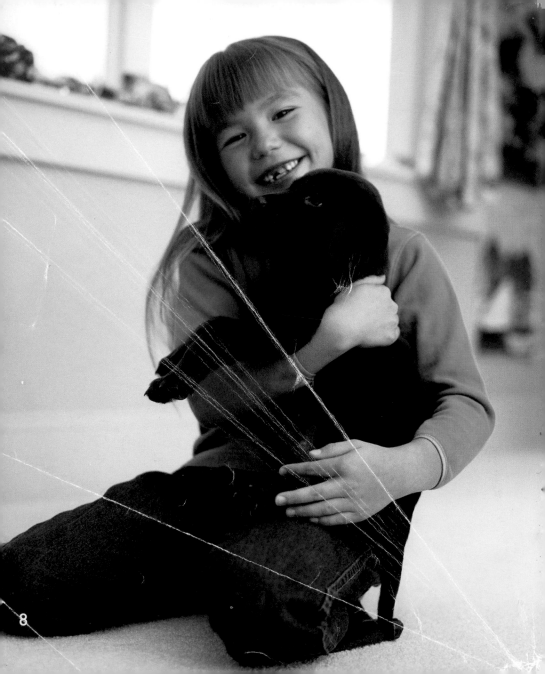

From Puppy to Adult

Lab puppies love to play.
They are gentle
and friendly with kids.

Lab puppies can be black, chocolate brown, or yellow. Some puppy litters are all one color. Some litters are mixed.

Adult Labs have strong bodies. Their short coats are waterproof. Their long tails and webbed toes help them swim.

Taking Care of Labs

Labs are big dogs that need a lot of exercise. Owners should take Labs on long walks every day. Labs like to play hard every day too.

Labs like lots of activity.
Owners can train them
for dog shows.
Labs can learn to jump
over bars and crawl
through tunnels.

Labs' short coats are easy to care for. Owners should brush them once each week.

Labradors are
popular dogs.
When well cared for,
they are playful pets
for many years.

Glossary

activity—action or movement

coat—a dog's fur

dog show—a contest where judges pick the best dog in several events

fetch—to go after something and bring it back

litter—a group of animals born at the same time to one mother

loyal—faithful to one's family and friends

popular—liked by many people; the Labrador is the most popular breed in the United States.

waterproof—able to keep water out

webbed—having folds of skin that connect the toes

Moustaki, Nikki. *Labrador Retrievers.* Neptune City, N.J.: T.F.H. Publications, 2006.

Murray, Julie. *Labrador Retrievers.* Animal Kingdom. Edina, Minn.: Abdo, 2005.

Internet Sites

FactHound offers a safe, fun way to find Internet sites related to this book. All of the sites on FactHound have been researched by our staff.

Here's how:

1. Visit *www.facthound.com*

2. Choose your grade level.

3. Type in this book ID **073686699X** for age-appropriate sites. You may also browse subjects by clicking on letters, or by clicking on pictures and words.

4. Click on the **Fetch It** button.

FactHound will fetch the best sites for you!

Index

brushing, 19
coats, 13, 19
color, 11
dog shows, 17
exercise, 15
fetching, 7
hunting, 7
kids, 9
litters, 11

owners, 15, 17, 19
pets, 5, 21
playing, 9, 15, 21
puppies, 9, 11
swimming, 13
tails, 13
training, 17
walks, 15
water, 7, 13

Word Count: 157
Grade: 1
Early-Intervention Level: 16

Editorial Credits
Martha E. H. Rustad, editor; Juliette Peters, set designer; Kyle Grenz, book designer;
Kara Birr, photo researcher; Scott Thoms, photo editor

Photo Credits
Ardea/Jean Michel Labat, 4; Capstone Press/Karon Dubke, 14, 18; Cheryl A. Ertelt, cover;
Corbis/George D. Lepp, 10; Kent Dannen, 16; Lynn M. Stone, 6; Photo by Fiona Green, 20;
Photodisc/Ryan McVay, 8; Shutterstock/Tina Rencelj, 1, 12